JENNY and the
TENNIS NUT

YEARLING BOOKS are designed especially to entertain and enlighten young people. Charles F. Reasoner, Professor of Elementary Education, New York University, is consultant to this series.

For a complete listing of all Yearling titles, write to Education Sales Department, Dell Publishing Co., Inc., 1 Dag Hammarskjold Plaza, New York, New York 10017.

JENNY and the TENNIS NUT

by
JANET
SCHULMAN

pictures by
MARYLIN
HAFNER

A Yearling Book

Published by
Dell Publishing Co., Inc.
1 Dag Hammarskjold Plaza
New York, New York 10017

ISBN: 0-440-44211-7

Reprinted by arrangement with Greenwillow Books
(a division of William Morrow and Company, Inc.)

Printed in the United States of America
First Yearling printing—May 1981

CW

For Lester, my favorite tennis nut
—J.S.

For my father,
who helped me find my game
—M. H.

Jenny stood on her hands.

"Fifty-eight, fifty-nine, sixty,"

she counted.

Just then her father

came into the room.

"Look at me, Daddy.

It is my best handstand yet,"

she said.

"What's so great about it?"
asked her father.
She looked at him upside down
and said, "I have been standing
like this for a minute."

"Well, I have been standing
like this for much longer.
About thirty-five years,"
said her father.
"Get yourself right side up.
I have a surprise for you."
He gave her a long,
funny-looking package.

"It looks like a tennis racket
and it feels like a tennis racket,"
said Jenny.
She tore off the paper.
"Big surprise.
It is a tennis racket,"
she said.

"Well, what do you say?"
asked her father.
"I don't know how to play tennis,"
said Jenny.
"I am going to teach you
and this will be your racket,"
he said.

Jenny picked up the racket.
"Hold it as if you were
shaking hands with a friend.
That is the right way to hold
a tennis racket," he said.
Jenny shook hands with the racket.
It did not feel like a friend.

"What if I don't like tennis?"
she asked.
"Oh, Jenny," said her father.
"You are going to love tennis.
I love tennis.

Your mama loves tennis.
And you will love tennis, too."

But Jenny was not listening.
She was balancing the racket
on the tip of her nose.
"Look, I'm a seal
playing tennis,"
she said.

Crash! The racket fell.
"You will break your racket.
It is not a toy," said her father.

"But, Daddy, did you see

what I did?" Jenny asked.

"I bet I could get real good

at being a tennis-playing seal."

Her father grinned.

"I bet you could get real good

at being a tennis-playing girl."

He picked up his racket
and some tennis balls.
"Come on outside, Jenny.
Let's give it a try.

We can hit the ball
against the side of the house,"
he said.
He drew a line with chalk
across the wall.

"Pretend that this line
 is the top of the net," he said.
"Some net. I can't jump over it
 when I win," said Jenny.

"First things first, Jenny.

First learn to hit the ball.

Like this," he said.

Thonk went the ball.
He hit a forehand stroke
and a backhand stroke
and a serve.

He hit the ball
again and again.

Bounce, hit.

Bounce, hit.

Bounce, hit.

19

He huffed and he puffed.

But he did not mind.

He loved hitting a tennis ball.

He loved it so much

that he forgot about teaching Jenny.

But she did not mind.
She was doing cartwheels
on the grass.

At last he stopped.

"Now you try," he said.

He threw a ball to her.

Swish went her racket.

"Keep your eye on the ball

and you won't miss," he said.

He threw another ball to her.

She kept her eye on the ball.

Zing went the ball over the fence
and into Mrs. Wister's yard.

"I'll get the ball," said Jenny.
She took a running start
and jumped up, up
and over Mrs. Wister's fence.

"That was pretty good,"
said her father. Jenny smiled.

"Oh, I can jump a lot higher
than that," she said.

"I meant that you hit
the ball pretty well," he said.
"Oh," she said.

Jenny jumped back over the fence.
"Then why did the ball go sideways
into Mrs. Wister's yard?" she asked.
"Because you were facing
the wall —I mean the net.

Always stand with your side
toward the net," he said.
"That is the right way
to stand when you hit the ball."

Jenny made a face.

"There are too many

rights and wrongs

in tennis," she said.

"Don't worry.

It will all come naturally,"

he said.

He threw a ball to her.

She kept her eye on the ball.

She stood with her side
toward the net.

She swung the racket.

Thonk went the ball.

"That's great!" said her father.

"You will be a winner

like Billie Jean King

in no time."

He grinned.

"Oh, Daddy, stop kidding,"

she said.

"Don't you want to be

a great tennis player?"

he asked.

"No. I want to be
a great circus acrobat,"
she said.

"A circus acrobat!
There are not many circuses
looking for acrobats nowadays.

But there are lots of tennis courts
looking for tennis players.

You can play tennis anywhere.
Think what fun we will have!"
he said.

"You mean think what fun
   you will have," she said.

"Oh, Jenny," he said.

"I just want you to have a sport
   you can do well and enjoy.
   That's why I want to teach you tennis."

She shook her head sadly.

"You have a one-track mind.

Tennis, tennis, tennis.

Oh, Daddy," she said.

"You are a tennis nut.

I already have a sport

I can do well and enjoy.

And I can do it

right in my own backyard.

Look!"

She ran to the grass.

She did four perfect cartwheels

and three somersaults.

Then she did a handstand
and a flip.

Her father watched her.

His eyes were wide open.

"Hey, that's good," he said.

"You haven't seen anything yet,"
she said.

"Now watch this."

She ran to the big oak tree
and stood on the old swing.

She swung higher
and higher and higher.

"Be careful," he said.

Just then she let go.

She flew through the air,

and landed on her feet.

Her father ran to her.

He looked worried.

"Are you all right, Jenny?"
he asked.

"Of course I'm all right, silly.
I do it all the time,"
she said.

"And I can climb ropes
just like the ladies
in the circus."

In no time she was up
the rope of the swing
and standing on the tree branch.

"And now, ladies and gentlemen,
the amazing Jennifer will do
her high wire act," she shouted.

Jenny began walking slowly
along the branch.

First right foot forward,
then left foot forward.

She held out her arms
to balance herself.

Her father looked up at her.

She looked very small.

He shut his eyes

and called, "Come down.

You will hurt yourself."

She slid down the rope.

Her father put his arm
around her.

"You are amazing, Jenny.
When did you learn
all those tricks?" he asked.

"On weekends.
When you and Mama
were playing tennis.
I was bored
so I played circus,"
she said.

He looked up at the tree.

He pulled at the rope.

"I am going to take down
this old swing," he said.

"Oh, no, Daddy!
Please don't do that,"
she cried.
"And I am going to put up
some real gymnastic equipment.
Some rings and a bar
and a nice soft mat under them.
And maybe a balance beam
closer to the ground
than that old tree branch,"
he said.

Jenny ran to her father
and threw her arms around him.
"You mean it's okay
for me to do my tricks?" she asked.

"It's more than okay.

I want you to.

You have found your game

all by yourself.

You do it well and

you really enjoy it.

Gymnastics is right for you,"

he said.

"Just like tennis is right for you.

Right?" she said.

"Right!" he answered.

They were both happy.

Jenny looked up at her father.

"There is something else, Daddy.

He picked up his racket
and a ball.

Bounce, hit.

Bounce, hit.

Bounce, hit.

There was no question
what his game was.

In a few minutes
Jenny came out again.
She did a flip
and watched her father
hit the ball.
At last he stopped.
"Maybe when you are older
you will want a second game,"
he said.
"I'll always be ready
to teach you tennis
when you are ready to learn."

"Okay," said Jenny.

"And if you ever want
a second game, I'll always be ready
to teach you cartwheels and flips.
You would love it."

And she grinned at him
upside down.

MS READ-a-thon— a simple way to start youngsters reading

Boys and girls between 6 and 14 can join the MS READ-a-thon and help find a cure for Multiple Sclerosis by reading books. And they get two rewards — the enjoyment of reading, and the great feeling that comes from helping others.

Parents and educators: For complete information call your local MS chapter. Or mail the coupon below.

Kids can help, too!